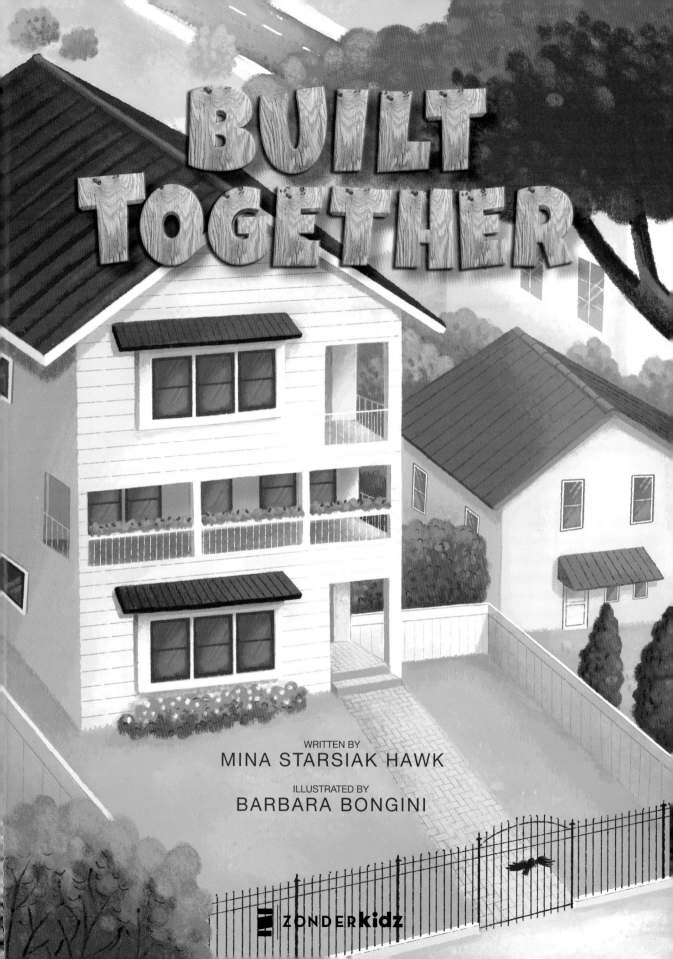

BUILT TOGETHER

WRITTEN BY
MINA STARSIAK HAWK

ILLUSTRATED BY
BARBARA BONGINI

ZONDERkidz

To my heart, Steve, Jack, and Charlie. I love you to the moon and back and cannot wait to continue building our family.
—MSH

I would like to dedicate this book to my family, the true pillar of my life.
—BB

ZONDERKIDZ

Built Together
Copyright © 2021 by Mina Starsiak Hawk
Illustrations © 2021 by Barbara Bongini

Requests for information
should be addressed to:

Zonderkidz, 3900 Sparks Dr. SE,
Grand Rapids, Michigan 49546

Hardcover ISBN 978-0-310-76928-6

Ebook ISBN 978-0-310-76929-3

Library of Congress Control Number: 2020941567

Art Direction and Design: Cindy Davis

Printed in Korea

21 22 23 24 25 26 27 28 / SAMHWA / 13 12 11 10 9 8 7 6 5 4 3 2 1

I live with just my mom and dad and our three goofy dogs, but we have a super big family.

I have 6 grandmas and grandpas, 10 uncles and aunts, 5 cousins, a bunch of step-grandmas, step uncles, and step-cousins, and lots of friends who Mom says might as well be family.

My mom says we're not related to everyone
by blood, even though I wish we were.
I'd really like to have freckles like Uncle Caz.

I've never seen Mom or Dad building our family. I wonder if they use a **hammer and nails?**

Or maybe a drill?

Or circular saw?

I wonder if Mom and Dad built our family with a **monkey wrench and pipes?**

Or
electrical wires?

And
tile and grout?

Maybe they use **paint and brushes?**

Or
mortar and bricks?

I want to help build our family too. I guess
I better ask which tools to use.

Mom says our family is built
with love and kindness.

By being there for the people we love when
they need us. And letting them be there for us too.

By celebrating the good stuff together.
And by helping each other with the tough stuff.

By including those who
might be overlooked.

And knowing that family
is not just made up of people.

Dad says we built our family by saying
"I'm sorry," and forgiving each other
when we've messed up.

By inviting our friends and
neighbors to be part of our family
and community every day.

And by happily joining in when others invite us.

Dad says you build a family by
making sure no one ever has to go
it alone if they don't want to.

**But having a hammer and nails
on hand never hurts!**